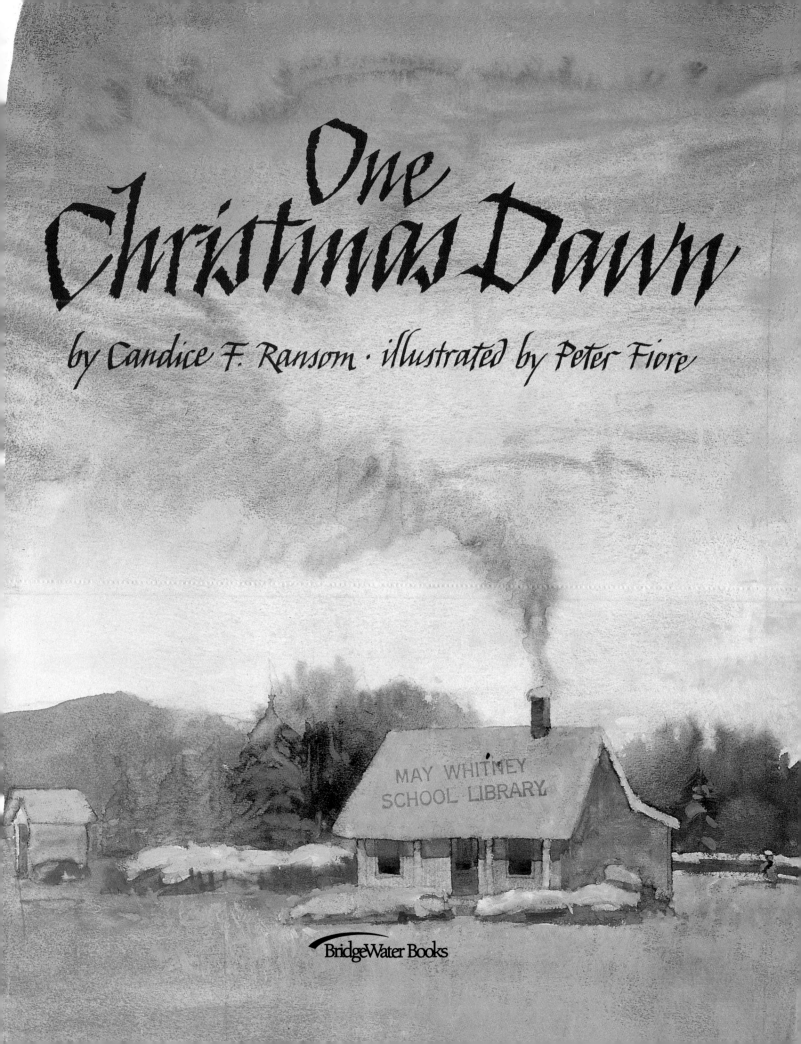

One Christmas Dawn

by Candice F. Ransom · illustrated by Peter Fiore

BridgeWater Books

Published by BridgeWater Paperback,
an imprint and trademark of Troll Communications L.L.C.

First printed in hardcover by BridgeWater Books.

First paperback edition published 1997.

Printed in Mexico

10 9 8 7 6 5 4 3

Library of Congress Cataloging-in-Publication Data

Ransom, Candice F.
One Christmas Dawn / by Candice F. Ransom;
illustrated by Peter Fiore.
p.   cm.
Summary: When her father has to leave their mountain
home to go to work in the city one cold winter, a ten-year-old
girl sees a special sign as she waits for his return on Christmas.
ISBN 0-8167-3384-8 (lib. bdg.) ISBN 0-8167-3385-6 (pbk.)
[1. Christmas – Fiction.   2. Mountain life – Virginia –
Fiction.   3. Virginia – Fiction.]   1. Fiore, Peter, ill.   II. Title.
PZ7.R1743On   1995   [E] – dc20   93-39751

In memory of my Highland grandparents.
CFR

Whenever I hear a train whistle, far off and low,
it puts me in mind of the girl I was, growing up in the mountains,
and the winter it was almost too cold for Christmas.
Back then we lived on Morning Star Ridge,
where Big Lick Creek turkey-tailed into three forks.
Daddy used to joke we were so far back in the hills,
we had to break day with an ax.

Daddy worked at the Pine Grove limestone quarry.
He walked there every day.
Sometimes he rode the train all the way to Bristol,
over mountains, across creeks on high-up trestle bridges.
Nobody else in our family had ever been out and beyond.
Not Mama, not my sister, not me.
The mountains held us in, like hands.

Near our place was a gravestone with no name,
only the words "Gone but."
The carver had meant to inscribe "Gone but not forgotten"
before running out of room.
I used to perch on the "Gone but" stone and wait
for the twice-daily train to come winding through the hills.
The people on the train were going yon side,
to faraway places.
I craved to be one of them.

The autumn I turned ten,
squirrels frazzled themselves burying acorns.
The orange stripe on the woolly bear's back was very narrow.
Signs of a hard winter, Daddy allowed.

One morning I broke a skin of ice on the water bucket.
Frost ferns were sketched on the windowpanes.
Big Lick froze solid, white as marble.
Day after day, the thermometer seemed stuck at zero.
Daddy claimed he had to thaw our words by the fire
before he could hear them!
Just before Christmas, he came home early from the quarry
and set his dinner pail on the table.

The men had been sent home, he said.
It was too cold to work.
He took the Bristol train to Three Springs,
where the sawmill was still running.
He got hired on, but it was too far for him to trot back and forth.
"Look for me at Christmas," he promised.
"I'll be home then."

It was too cold to sit on my "Gone but" stone
and watch for the train,
but each day I listened for the whistle.

Then one day I didn't hear the train.
"Too cold for the Bristol to run," Mama said.
The whole world stood motionless,
frozen by the cold.
"Will Daddy make it home for Christmas?" I asked my sister.
"I don't know," she said.

Every Christmas Eve, we'd have a big dinner,
then play Old Granny Gobble.
On Christmas morning, we'd have oyster stew
and open our presents.
But without Daddy, it wouldn't be Christmas.

On Christmas Eve, I hung my stocking by the fireplace.
My sister hung hers, too, even though she was nearly grown.
"Come put your feet under the board," Mama called.
She had been cooking the day long.
Supper was a treat: ham hocks and shucky-beans;
light bread; and my favorite, stack cake.
But I couldn't eat much.
After supper we played Old Granny Gobble.
I won. But it wasn't any fun without Daddy.

"Let's go out," said my sister.
She'd heard tell that if a single girl visited the hogpen
on Christmas Eve, she'd see her future husband.
The hogs were huddled in the straw.
"That old fat boar grunted at you," I teased.
"He didn't, neither," she said. " 'Twas the young shoat."
She wasn't about to have an old, fat husband.

The stars were brittle chips of ice.
My breath chuffed in frosty puffs like steam from the train.
Will my daddy come home? I asked the stars silently.
Then my sister grabbed my hand, and we raced
through the diamond-bright cold to the house.

Mama bundled quilts on our bed.
"Nighty-night," she said and kissed my cheek.
My sister fell asleep, but I lay awake for hours.
I waited and waited for the familiar whistle.
Where was the train?

A strange glow at the window caught my eye.
I tiptoed across the cold floor to see.
Outside was the most wondrous sight!

Light chased the cold darkness clean from the sky.
A fireball flamed over the ridge—the sun, hot as July!
Before my eyes, elder and oak,
pokeweed and laurel sprouted buds.
By the porch, Mama's rose of Sharon bush unfurled
and grew like Jack's beanstalk.
Trees and plants shed ice cocoons.
Flowers popped out of winter-blackened stumps.
The world was touched with summer.

Far off, I heard the whistle of the Bristol train,
chugging through the holler like a promise.
I looked at the clock. The train wasn't late.
It was an hour early!

And then, quick as it appeared, the sun sank below the ridge.
Leaves dropped off the trees. Plants withered and died.
The holler was cold and dark again.
I don't recollect going back to bed.
The next thing I remember, my sister was shaking me.
"Get up, sleepyhead. It's Christmas!"
Cloudy dawn crept through the window.
Had I only dreamed the sun had thawed our ice-locked holler?

I climbed out of bed and ran downstairs.
And there was Daddy, warming his hands by the stove.
"Merry Christmas," he said.
"How did you get here?" I asked.
He winked. "I found a way."
Crisp, foreign air clung to his clothes,
the smell of sidewalks and city stores.
He pulled a jar from his pocket.
"Wouldn't be Christmas without oyster stew," he said.

There were presents, too.
A cedar notion box for my sister.
For me, a store-bought doll with real hair and china-blue eyes—
not a playing-with doll but a looking-at doll.
"I got her in Bristol," Daddy said.
But I knew that, just like I knew how Daddy got home.
The doll was a sign, I thought,
from yon side the hills to me.
Someday I'd see the city for myself.
But for now, the important thing was
we were all together.

Years later, I left the holler on the Bristol train.
The mountains parted before me like hands unclasping.
I never sat on my "Gone but" stone again.
But whenever a train whistle blows, far off and low,
I remember that magic Christmas I was ten,
when the sun rose in the night,
and Mama's rose of Sharon bush bloomed.

Days gone, but not forgotten.

AUTHOR'S NOTE

The winter of 1917, the inspiration for this story, was one of the coldest on record in the mountains of southwest Virginia. Temperatures remained below zero for weeks. When the spring thaw finally came, melting ice flooded the creeks and washed away many homes.

People in the mountains often read "signs" to predict the weather or a person's future. Visiting the hogpen on Christmas Eve was a way a single girl might "see" her future husband. If an old, fat hog grunted at her first, she would marry an old, fat man. If a shoat—a young hog—grunted at her, her husband would be young and handsome.

The game Old Granny Gobble was popular on long winter nights. The object of the game was to try to drum both fists on your knees and both feet on the floor—which was called beating all four "hammers"—while you nodded your head at the same time. Try it!

The story of the early Christmas dawn, handed down among the mountain folk, may be traced back to the British legend of the Glastonbury rose, which is said to bloom an hour before the true dawn on old Christmas Day, January 6.